Paws, Claws, Hands, and Feet
By Kimberly Hutmacher
Illustrated By Sherry Rogers

Waking, shaking,
feel the beat,
paws, claws,
hands, and feet . . .

Digging, dashing,
acorn stashing . . .

Curling, clinging,
tree branch swinging . . .

Prowling, peeking,
crumblies seeking . . .

The Big Book
of BUGS

Spinning, swooping,
picture looping . . .

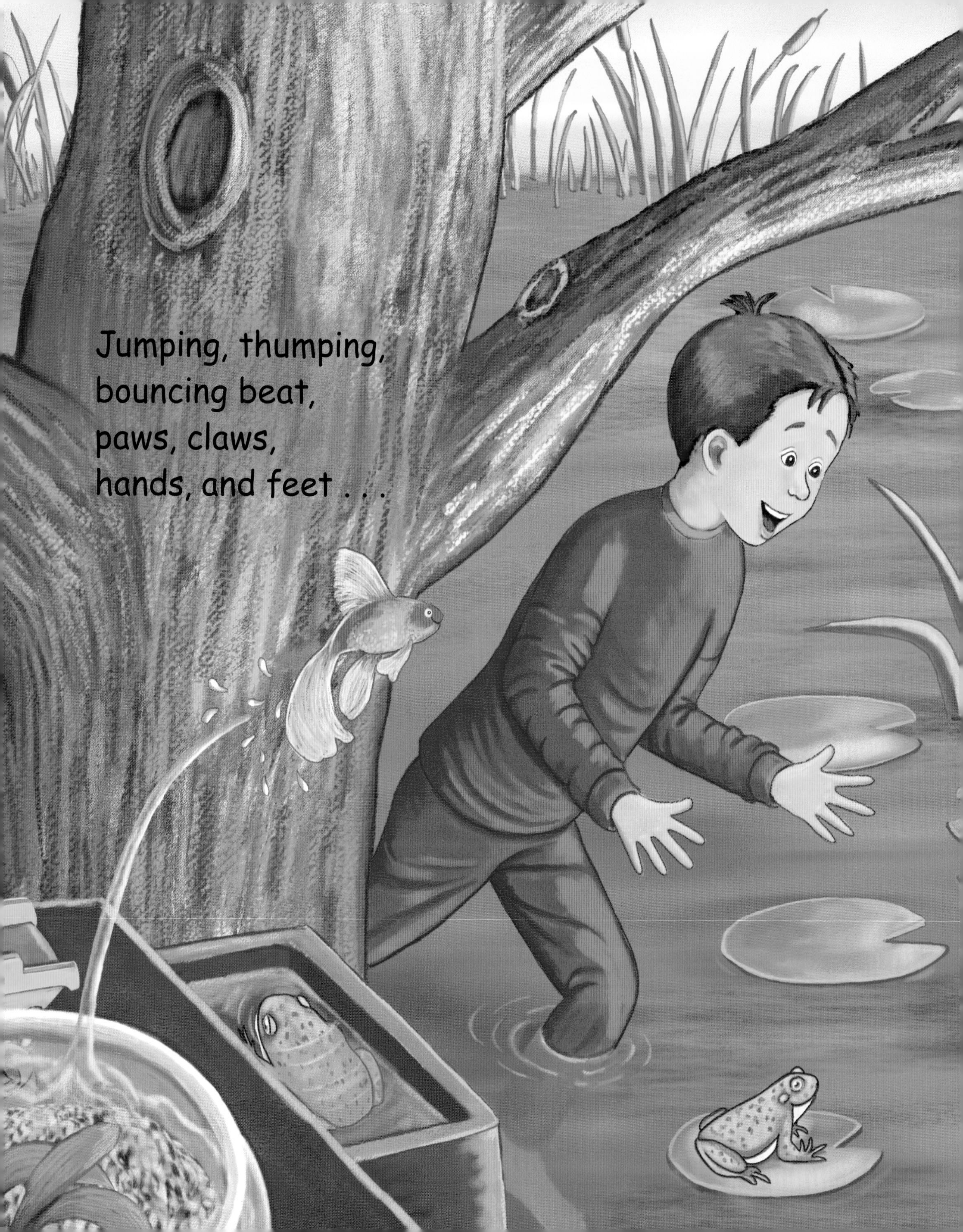

Jumping, thumping,
bouncing beat,
paws, claws,
hands, and feet . . .

Leaping, lunging,
lily pad plunging . . .

Dipping, dashing,
iceberg splashing . . .

Roaming, romping,
prairie stomping . . .

Hipping, hopping,
outback bopping . . .

Lazing, pacing,
slow the beat,
paws, claws,
hands, and feet . . .

Clutching, clawing,
homestead pawing . . .

Crawling, creeping,
time for sleeping . . .

Rounding, resting,
pillow nesting . . .

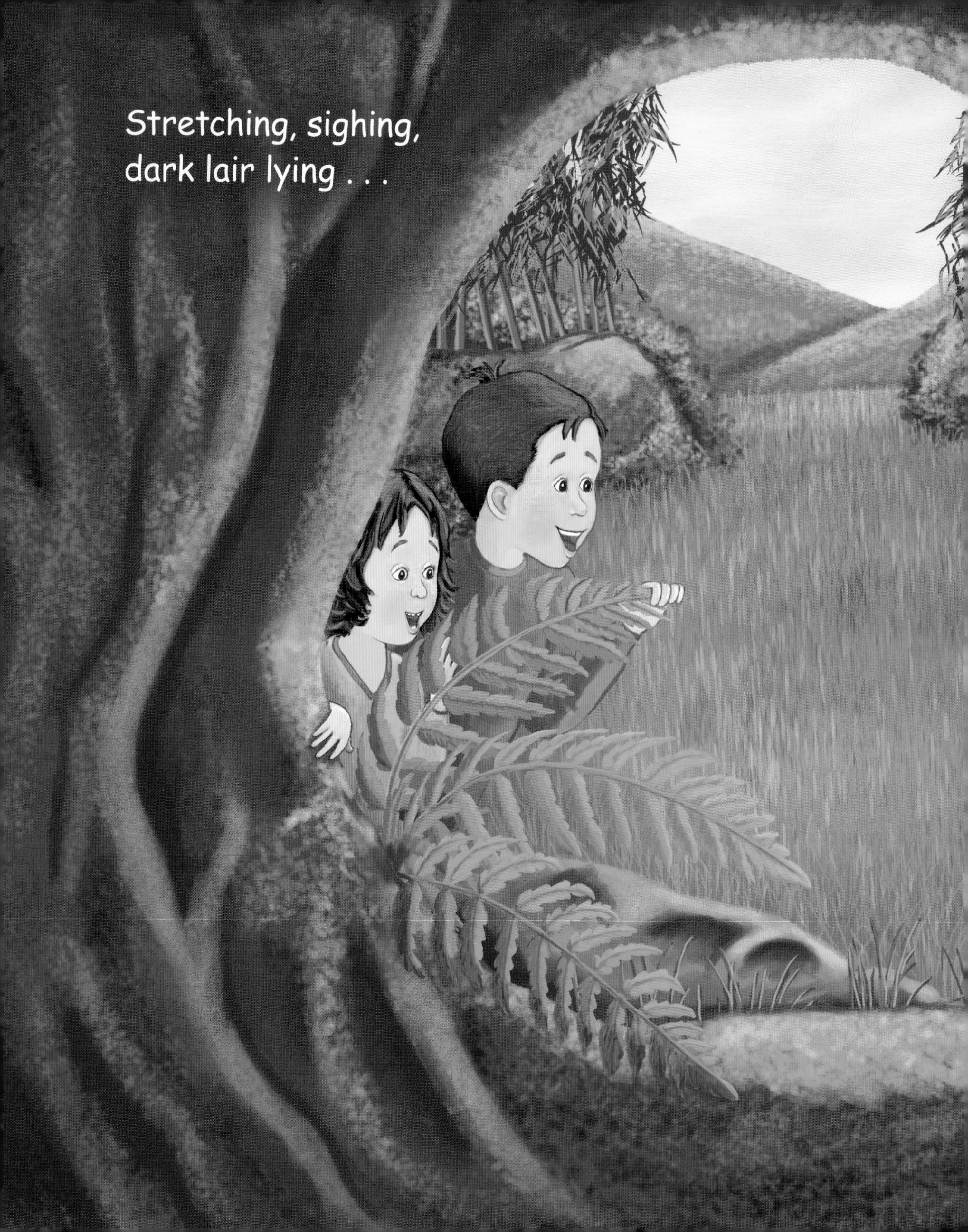
Stretching, sighing,
dark lair lying . . .

ABC Safari
In Arctic Waters
Turtles In My Sandbox
If You Were A Parrot
One Odd Day
Happy Birthday To Whooo?
Tudley Didn't Know
Octavia and Her Purple Ink Cloud
The Giraffe Who Was Afraid of Heights
If A Dolphin Were A Fish
Loon Chase
How The Moon Regained Her Shape
Christmas Eve Blizzard
Pieces of Another World
Water Beds
Carolina's Sto
Claws, Paws, Hands and Feet
Whistling Wings
Sort it Out!
Saturn for my Birthday
Riverbeds
My Half Day
Blackberry Banquet
Kersplatypus
Animals Are Sleeping
The Best Nest
T'was the Day Before Zoo
My Even Day
Julie The Rockhound
Little Skink's Tail
A Day in the Salt Marsh
Burro's Tortillas
In My Backyard
Ocean Seasons
The Rainforest Grew
Turtle Summer

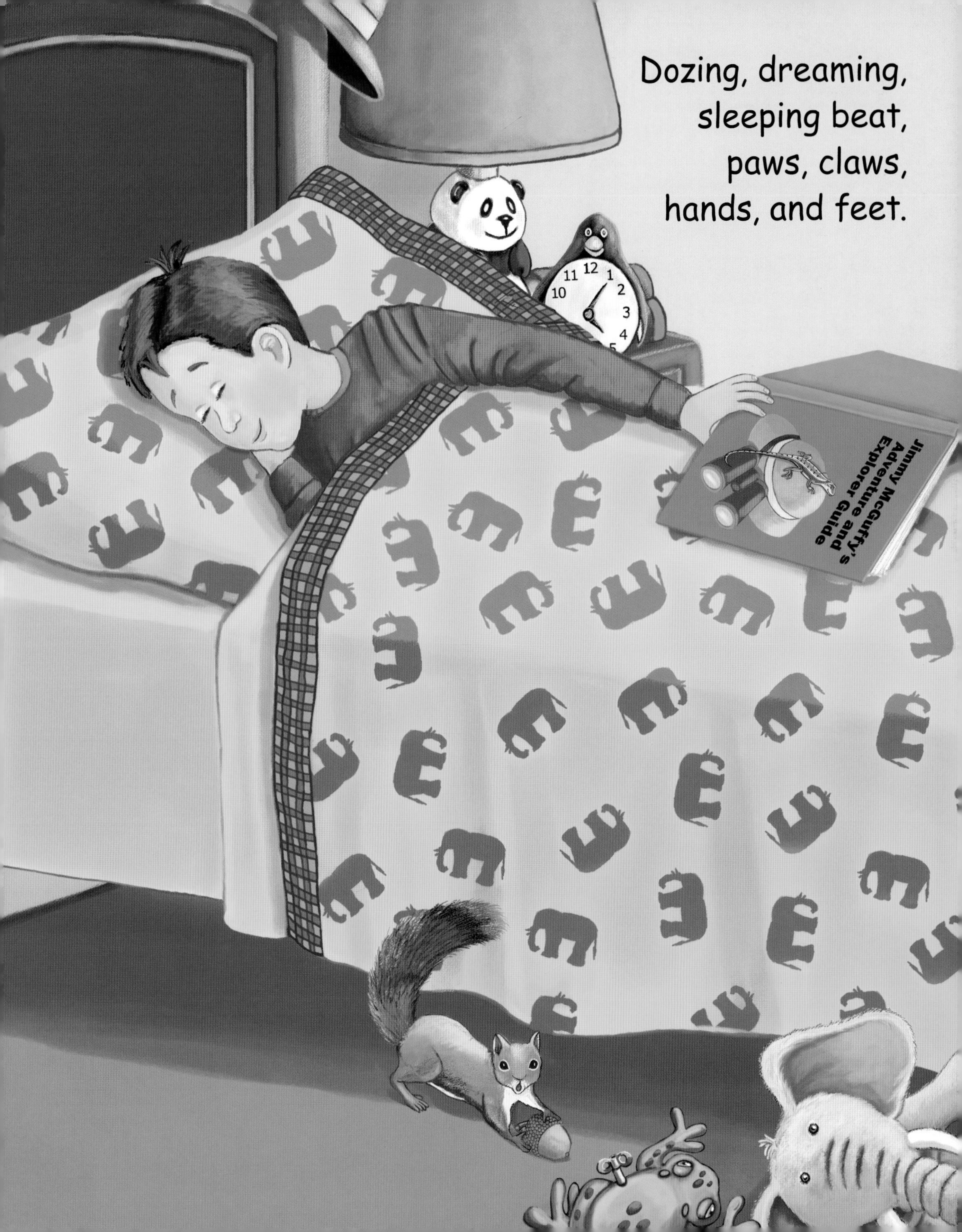

Dozing, dreaming,
sleeping beat,
paws, claws,
hands, and feet.

Paws, Claws, Hands, and Feet Matching Activity

Solve the riddle and match the information to the animals' paws, claws, hands, or feet. Answers are upside down on the bottom of the next page.

a. Elephant

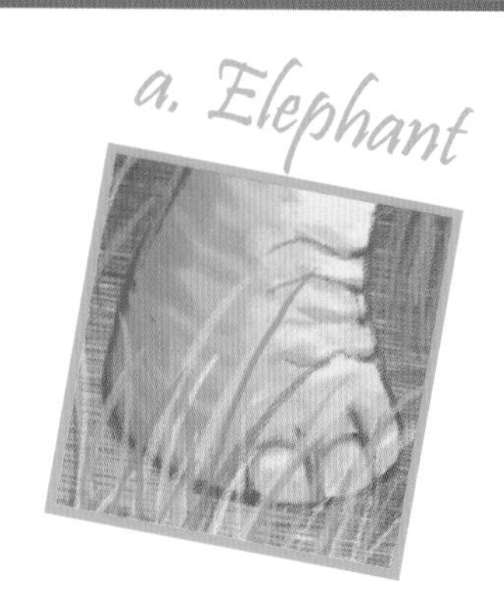

1 This familiar backyard animal with a bushy tail has five toes on its hind feet and four toes with strong claws on its front feet. It can run but not very fast. It relies on agility for climbing trees, jumping, and hiding to escape enemies. To cool itself off, it sweats from the pads of its feet! You may see little wet footprints on a hot day.

b. Rat

2 This small rodent has sharp claws attached to short, stubby legs. It uses the claws to forage for food and can move very fast.

c. Tortoise

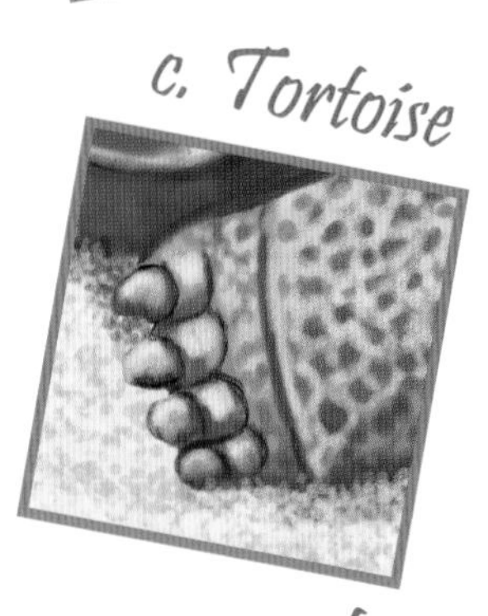

3 This huge mammal's feet are large and well padded to help it walk quietly. Each foot has five toes, but we can only see the three toes that have toenails. The feet and columnar legs help this very heavy animal stand for long periods of time.

d. Squirrel

4 This reptile carries protection on its back. Some people believe this shell can be taken off, but that is not true — the spine is connected to the inside of the shell. Short, stumpy, muscular legs support its heavy body, and claws on its feet allow this animal to dig in all types of soil.

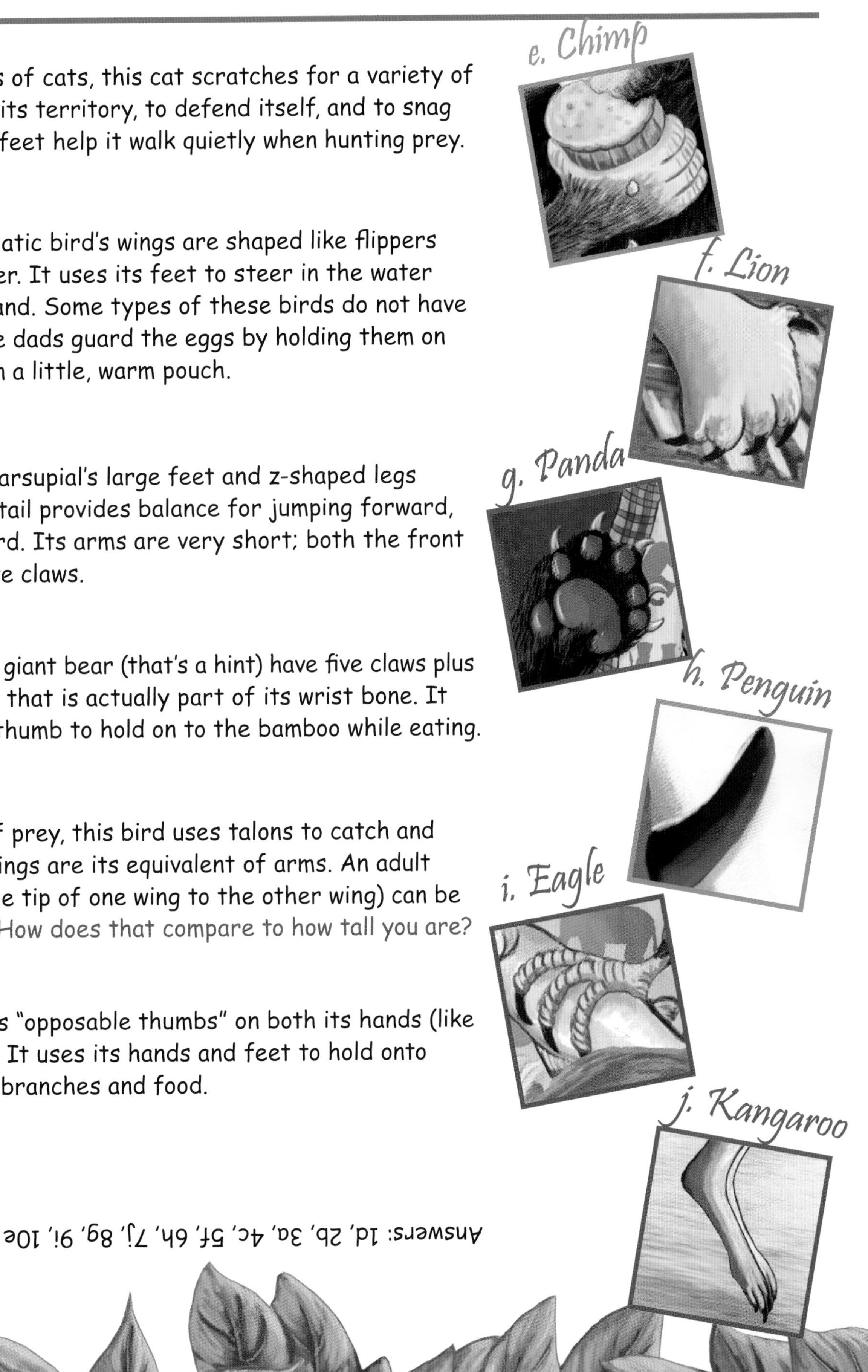

5 Just like all types of cats, this cat scratches for a variety of reasons: to mark its territory, to defend itself, and to snag prey. Its padded feet help it walk quietly when hunting prey.

6 This flightless, aquatic bird's wings are shaped like flippers to swim in the water. It uses its feet to steer in the water and to waddle on land. Some types of these birds do not have nests. Instead, the dads guard the eggs by holding them on top of their feet in a little, warm pouch.

7 This Australian marsupial's large feet and z-shaped legs help it jump. The tail provides balance for jumping forward, rather than upward. Its arms are very short; both the front and back feet have claws.

8 The hands of this giant bear (that's a hint) have five claws plus a special "thumb" that is actually part of its wrist bone. It uses this special thumb to hold on to the bamboo while eating.

9 Like most birds of prey, this bird uses talons to catch and hold onto prey. Wings are its equivalent of arms. An adult wingspan (from the tip of one wing to the other wing) can be six to eight feet. How does that compare to how tall you are?

10 This primate has "opposable thumbs" on both its hands (like we do) and feet. It uses its hands and feet to hold onto things like tree branches and food.

Answers: 1d, 2b, 3a, 4c, 5f, 6h, 7j, 8g, 9i, 10e

Hands and Feet — what are they good for?

Your feet

How many feet do you have?

How many toes do you have on each foot?

Are your toes the same length?

Think of things we do with our feet.

Can you pick up something with your toes?

What part of your foot touches the ground first when you walk or run?

Can you stand on your toes?

Your hands

How many hands do you have?

How many fingers do you have on each hand?

What do you notice about your thumbs?

Can you cut a piece of paper with scissors without using your thumb?

Try picking something up and holding it without using your thumb!

Do all animals have feet?
How are the animals' feet similar to or different than your feet?
If an animal doesn't have any feet, how does it move?
How do some animals use feet to move?
What else do they do with their feet?
What animals have two feet or four feet?
How are the animals' hands similar to or different than your hands?
Why do some animals have wings instead of arms or hands?
Why do some animals have flippers instead of hands or feet?

Paws, Claws, Hands, and Feet Adaptations

Match the paws, claws, hands, and feet to the adaptations for which they are used:

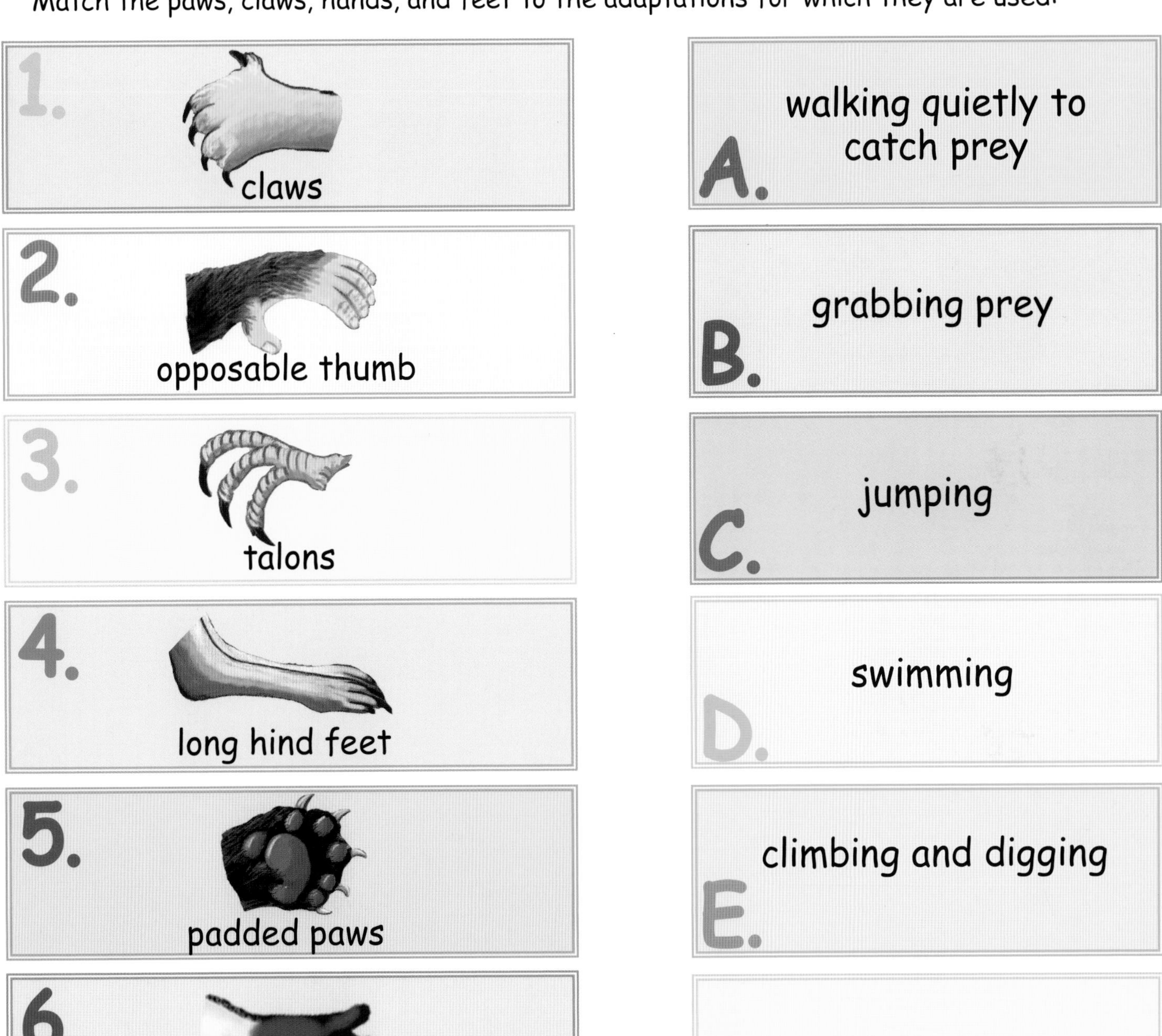

What other animals do you know that have similar paws, claws, hands, or feet as those above?

Answers: 1. e, 2. f, 3. b, 4. c, 5. a, 6. d

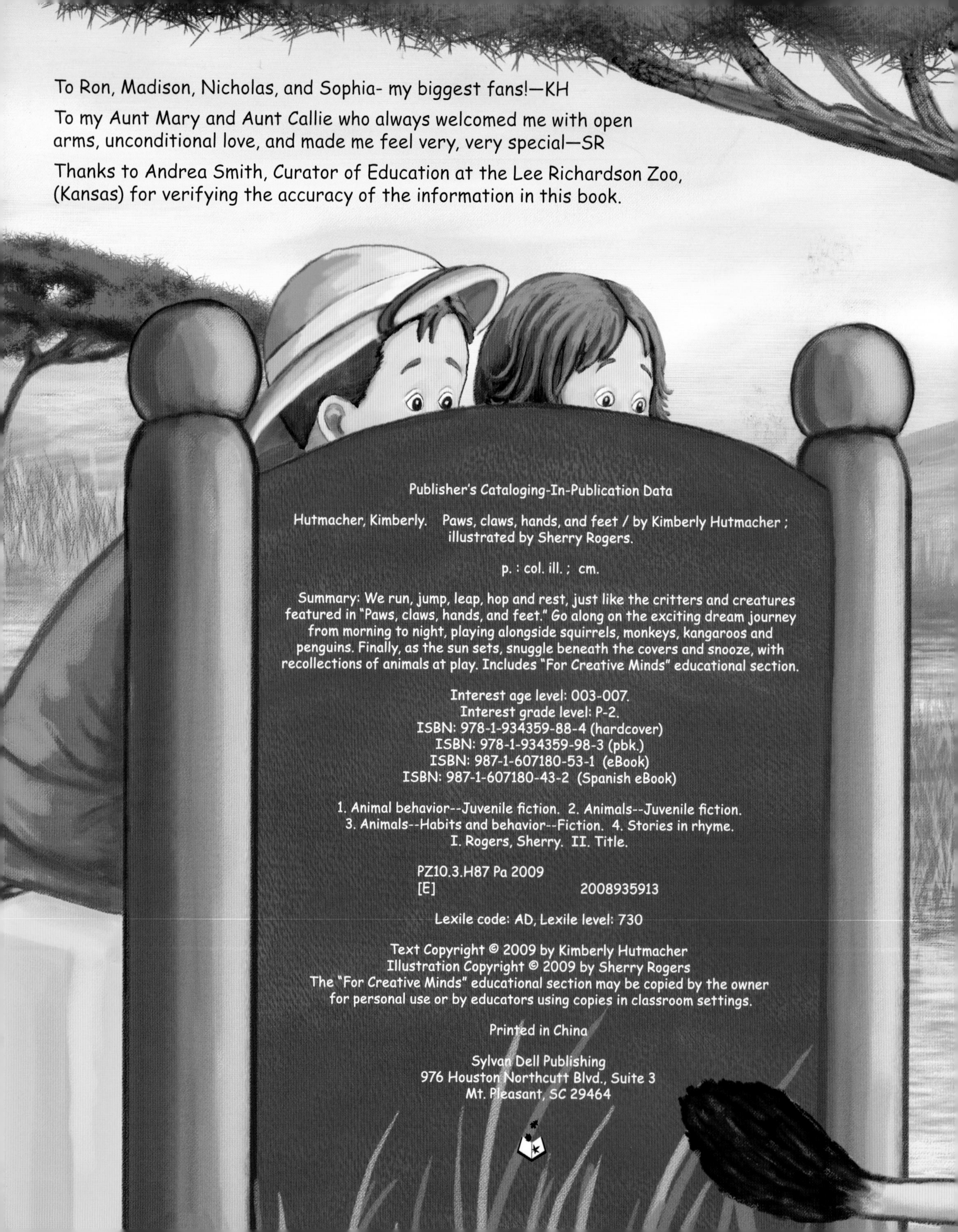

To Ron, Madison, Nicholas, and Sophia- my biggest fans!—KH

To my Aunt Mary and Aunt Callie who always welcomed me with open arms, unconditional love, and made me feel very, very special—SR

Thanks to Andrea Smith, Curator of Education at the Lee Richardson Zoo, (Kansas) for verifying the accuracy of the information in this book.

Publisher's Cataloging-In-Publication Data

Hutmacher, Kimberly. Paws, claws, hands, and feet / by Kimberly Hutmacher ; illustrated by Sherry Rogers.

p. : col. ill. ; cm.

Summary: We run, jump, leap, hop and rest, just like the critters and creatures featured in "Paws, claws, hands, and feet." Go along on the exciting dream journey from morning to night, playing alongside squirrels, monkeys, kangaroos and penguins. Finally, as the sun sets, snuggle beneath the covers and snooze, with recollections of animals at play. Includes "For Creative Minds" educational section.

Interest age level: 003-007.
Interest grade level: P-2.
ISBN: 978-1-934359-88-4 (hardcover)
ISBN: 978-1-934359-98-3 (pbk.)
ISBN: 987-1-607180-53-1 (eBook)
ISBN: 987-1-607180-43-2 (Spanish eBook)

1. Animal behavior--Juvenile fiction. 2. Animals--Juvenile fiction. 3. Animals--Habits and behavior--Fiction. 4. Stories in rhyme. I. Rogers, Sherry. II. Title.

PZ10.3.H87 Pa 2009
[E] 2008935913

Lexile code: AD, Lexile level: 730

Printed in China

Sylvan Dell Publishing
976 Houston Northcutt Blvd., Suite 3
Mt. Pleasant, SC 29464